MORTIMER MOONER MAKES LUNCH

Written by Frank B. Edwards
Illustrated by John Bianchi

BUNGALO BOOKS

It was a bright summer morning when the Mooners slept in. "Jumping Red River Toads, you're late," cried Mortimer Mooner as he pushed his father out of bed. "You have TEN minutes to catch your bus."

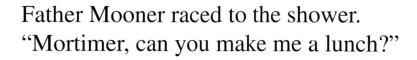

Father Mooner raced to the shower.
"Mortimer, can you make me a lunch?"

Father Mooner scrubbed his back and washed his hair. "NINE minutes and counting," called Mortimer as he got out the bread.

Father Mooner dried himself off and shaved his chin.
"EIGHT minutes to go," reported Mortimer as he
dashed to the refrigerator.

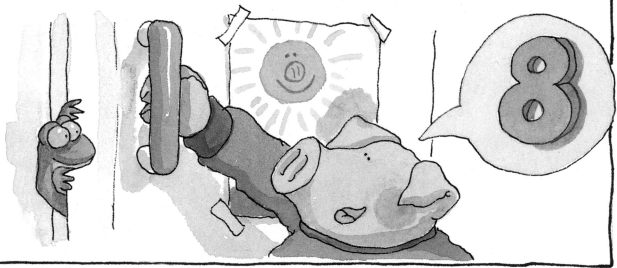

Father Mooner brushed his teeth and combed his hair.

"Only SEVEN minutes remaining," announced Mortimer as he opened the peanut butter jar.

Father Mooner pulled on his socks and hopped
to his closet.

"SIX minutes left," declared Mortimer Mooner.
"Are you dressed yet?" He added some pickles.

Father Mooner jumped into his pants and buttoned up his shirt.

"FIVE minutes," shouted Mortimer as he added some of his father's favourite cheese to the sandwich.

Father Mooner pulled on his shoes and rushed out of the bedroom.

"FOUR…" yelled Mortimer as he crammed the giant sandwich into a plastic bag.

Father Mooner snatched a bright red tie and his very best jacket.

"THREE…" hollered Mortimer as he grabbed some fruit and a juice box.

Father Mooner charged down the stairs and headed for the door.

"JUST TWO MINUTES LEFT," screamed Mortimer as he slipped some dessert into his father's briefcase.

"ONE…" thundered Mortimer
as he tossed Father Mooner his
briefcase and enormous lunch.

"…BLAST OFF!!!!"
Father Mooner caught his lunch and tripped over the morning newspaper. As the lunch and paper flew into the air, he bounced down the steps and landed with a thump!

"Oops," whispered Mortimer, lifting the paper from his father's face. "I think you're actually kind of early. You don't have to work today after all — it's Saturday. Maybe we can go on a picnic instead!"

"Good idea," groaned Father Mooner, getting to his feet. "But I'm not sure we can eat this huge lunch ourselves."

"Of course, we can…" said Mortimer Mooner.

"…we're pigs!"